The Pug in the Helmet

My first book for my first loves, Bertie, Florence and Mathilda (who came up with the idea and inspired the story of Phyllis and her helmet!)

Phyllis was a safety-conscious Pug.

She liked to wear a helmet, especially when she rode her bike to school.

In fact, Phyllis was so safety-conscious that she wore her helmet most of the time.

She wore it while she ate her dinner.

She wore it when she had a bath.

She even tried to wear it in bed, just in case she fell out.

She never did fall out, but Phyllis was a 'just in case' sort of Pug.

Wearing her helmet all the time did, however, come with one teeny, tiny problem.

Whenever Phyllis took off her helmet, she had the most incredible,

the most spectacular,

the most magnificent...
helmet hair!

It made her school friends laugh.

And that made Phyllis sad, and a little bit self-conscious.

But it didn't stop her riding her bike.

Or wearing her helmet.

Dad took Phyllis to the shops.
People looked quizzically at her wearing her helmet.

Dad said 'Phyllis love, why don't you take off the helmet?'

'Because just in case,' said Phyllis, which was lucky, because at
just that moment

a giant stack of tinned beans fell over as they walked past.
It missed them.

Just.

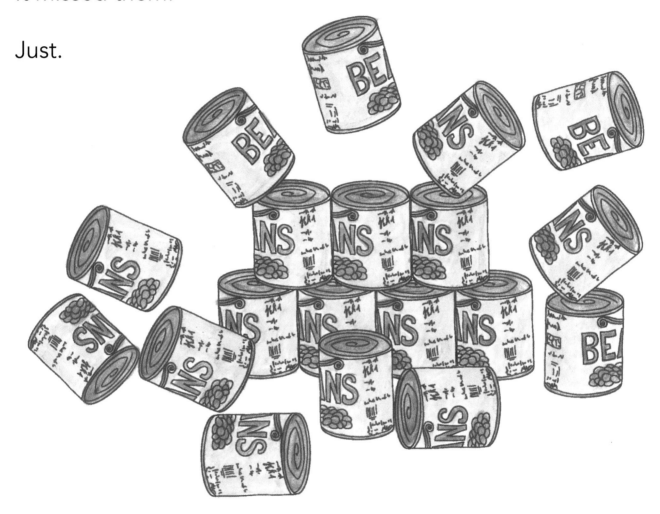

'You see?' said Phyllis.
'Hmm," said Dad.

They walked home with their bags of shopping. A can of bright orange paint fell from a ladder and landed on the pavement just in front of them.

Paint splashed all over the ground, up the wall, and even over Dad's brand new shoes.
'Botheration!' said Dad.

'At least it didn't land on our heads,' said Phyllis in a matter of fact sort of voice, and tapped her helmet, knowingly.

'Hmm,' said Dad.

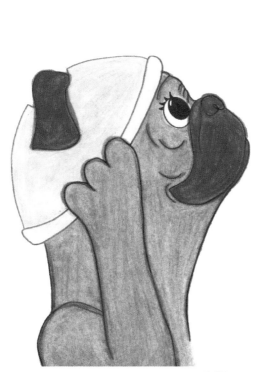

The next day, Phyllis got her bike out of the shed and started cycling to school. She met up with her friends along the way.

There was Neeta and Harold and Aggie and Brian.

Neeta and Harold and Aggie and Brian didn't wear helmets when they rode their bikes.

They didn't wear them when they were eating their dinner, having a bath, or even when they were in bed.

They said they didn't want helmet hair. Phyllis thought helmet hair was a small price to pay for safety. Because, you know, just in case.

They cycled along, enjoying the morning sun, chatting about the games they were going to play at break time.

Neeta and Brian enjoyed tag, running around and making each other 'it'.

Harold and Aggie liked playing 'explorers' and were excited about what they might find behind the timber trail that day.

Phyllis enjoyed both games equally, just so long as they were played safely.

None of the pups were really paying much attention to the road. Suddenly a cat ran out in front of Harold. He swerved his bike to avoid hitting the cat. But he hit the pavement instead and toppled over.

Aggie's bike flew into Harold's, did a somersault, and landed on top of him. So did Aggie.

Neeta swerved to the right, clipped Aggie's wheel, and fell over.

Brian pulled hard on his brakes, skidded onto his side, and then collided with Neeta.

Phyllis stopped her bike just in time to see the jumble of her friends and their bikes on the road in front of her.

Neeta and Harold and Aggie and Brian had bumps and bruises on their heads. An ambulance arrived and a medic helped clean them up, putting on bandages and plasters.

They were told they were very lucky it hadn't been worse.

The friends all sat on the grass next to their bikes, feeling very sorry for themselves.

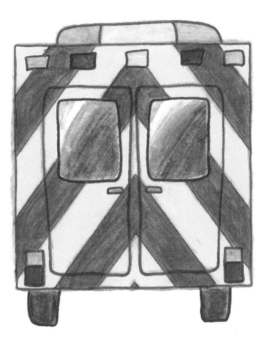

Watching the ambulance disappear up the road, Phyllis knew what she had to do.

Very slowly, she undid the chin strap and lifted her helmet off her head. She turned dramatically, to face her friends.

There, glowing in the morning light was her most splendid,

her most extraordinary,

her most impressive helmet hair!

'Ta-dah!' she shouted.

Her friends blinked in the sunlight.
They looked at her hair.
They looked at each other.

And then they laughed!

They laughed so hard they almost forgot about all their aches and pains. Almost, just for a moment.

Phyllis laughed too.
'Helmet hair rules!' shouted Brian!

'I wish I had helmet hair rather than these bandages!' said Aggie!

They all agreed helmet hair was a lot more preferable to bumps and bruises. And it looked pretty cool too.

The next day, the friends all wore their helmets to school.

When they arrived, they took them off, laughing together as they proudly admired each others' hair.

They all had...

the most tremendous,

the most astonishing,

the most outstanding helmet hair!

But Phyllis's was the most spectacular of all!

About the Author

Laura Storey

Laura is first and foremost mum to three beautiful children, Bertie (the most polite, considerate teenager in the world), Flo-flo (an illustrator and architect in the making) and Mathilda (who fills the world with song and crazy dancing). Second to family she works for a global company as an Employee Communications Leader and takes every opportunity to include poetry and fun rhymes into her work. Laura is also a diversity and inclusion ally in all aspects of her life; she understands how critical it is to support children so they can grow up to be the most authentic version of themselves, however they identify. Her children are the idea-generators behind the stories she's currently writing because honestly, who knows better what to write for children, than children themselves?

Visit www.laurastorey.com for more information.

About the Illustrator

Melissa Muldoon

Melissa is an artist, sculptor and illustrator. Inspired hugely by nature and our beautiful planet, obsessed with making the world a prettier place and bringing imagination to life. Melissa always has numerous projects on the go at any one time, she illustrates books, runs children's art workshops, builds sculptures (mostly out of pre-loved materials) for community projects and private commissions, and works in graphic/logo design in her 'spare' time.
Previous illustrated books include The Mouse's House, Mouse's Best Day Ever, Mouse And The Storm, T-Rex to Chicken and Moonlight in the Garden. Still in the pipeline are numerous mindful books, illustrated works for poetry and some exciting plans with Laura Storey!

Visit www.melissamuldoon.co.uk for more information.

Printed in Great Britain
by Amazon

77831770R00027